5.95

DATE DUE			
DEC 7 - 8 NOV			
DEC 11 NOV 19			
SEP 27			
OCT 4 DEC 2			
OCT 29 FEB 1			
FEB 2 MAY T			
NOV 5			
SEP 2 DEC 1 6			
OCT 24			
NOV 14			
MAY 10			
SEP 18			

3839

F
ABE

Abels, Harriette S.

Mystery on Mars.

MYSTERY ON MARS

BY HARRIETTE S. ABELS

Library of Congress Cataloging in Publication Data

Abels, Harriette Sheffer.
  Mystery on Mars.
  (Galaxy I)
  SUMMARY: While visiting the Mars colony, the crew of Emergency
Spaceship EM 88 helps to rescue miners trapped by an earthquake and
discovers some unusual inhabitants deep in the mountain.
  (1. Science fiction) I. Title. II. Series.
PZ7.A1595Mv   (Fic)   79-9923
ISBN 0-89686-024-8

International Standard Book Numbers: Library of Congress
  0-89686-024-8 Library Bound   Catalog Card Number:
  0-89686-033-7 Paperback   79-9923

CRESTWOOD HOUSE

P.O. Box 3427
Hwy. 66 South
Mankato, MN 56001

MYSTERY ON MARS

BY HARRIETTE S. ABELS

ILLUSTRATED BY RODNEY
AND BARBARA FURAN

EDITED BY DR. HOWARD SCHROEDER

Professor in Reading and Language Arts
Dept. of Elementary Education
Mankato State University

3839

DESIGNED BY BARBARA FURAN

About the author . . .

Harriette Sheffer Abels was born December 1, 1926 in Port Chester, New York. She attended Furman University, Greenville, South Carolina for one year. In addition to having her poetry published in the Furman literary magazine, she had her first major literary success while at the University. She wrote, produced and directed a three act musical comedy that was a smash hit!

At the age of twenty she moved to California, where she worked as a medical secretary for four years. In September, 1949, she married Robert Hamilton Abels, a manufacturers sales representative.

She began writing professionally in September, 1963. Her first major story was published in **Highlights For Children** in March, 1964, and her second appeared in **Jack and Jill** a short while later. She has been selling stories and articles ever since. Her first book was published by Ginn & Co., for the Magic Circle Program, in 1970.

Harriette and her husband love to travel and are looking forward to their annual trip to Europe. While travel doesn't leave much time for writing, Harriette does try to write at least something every day. When at home a sunporch serves as her office, but she confesses that most of her serious writing is done while stretched out on her bed.

The Abels have three children - Barbara Heidi, David Mark, and Carol Susan, and three dogs - Coco, Bon Bon, and Ginger Ale.

MYSTERY ON MARS

The landing pad on planet Mars was clear. Emergency Spaceship EM 88 settled down easily and quietly. Brita, the pilot of the EM 88, switched off the power supply.

"All secure, Druce," she announced over the intertel. "Are you leaving the ship?"

The voice of the EM 88's captain came over the speaker. "I have a report to finish," he said. "But tell the crew they can visit the colony if they want to."

Joris, the co-pilot of the EM 88, switched on the ship's general intertel. "Attention," he called. "We have landed at the Mars colony. Any crew member wishing to leave may do so at this time. That is all."

Rina, the EM 88's navigator, came out of her small cubicle. "Are you two going into the colony?" she asked.

"We might as well," Brita said. "We're going to be docked here for several days. Druce has some business with the leader of the colony."

"I'll stay around here," Joris said. "Druce might need some help."

Brita and Rina left the ship and Joris closed up the pilot's cabin. He went from the third level down to the second and knocked on Druce's cabin door.

"Come in," Druce called.

"Can I help you, sir?" Joris asked as he walked into the room.

"Thank you, Joris." Druce looked up from the papers on his desk. "I don't think so. I should be finished in about an hour."

"Brita and Rina went over to the colony," Joris said.

"Fine," said Druce. "This should be an easy mission. The problem I've come to discuss with Tobit is about delivery of supplies. There won't be anything for the crew to do while we're here."

"Well, if you don't need me," Joris said, "I'll go see if Ivo wants to go into the colony."

He went down to the first level of the ship where the ship's engineer was busy repairing a small computer in his cabin.

"We have a few days with nothing to do," Joris said. "Brita and Rina have already left for the colony. Why don't we go, too?"

"I don't think so," Ivo said. "This will give me a good chance to catch up on some of these small jobs I've been putting off." He pointed to a broken computer. "I've been trying to get to this for weeks now."

A loud clicking came from the corner.

"What does Amorf want?" Joris asked.

Ivo went over, and picked up the pink amorphous blob that he kept as a pet. "What's your problem, Amorf?" he said.

The blob's computer kept on clicking. Ivo shook his head.

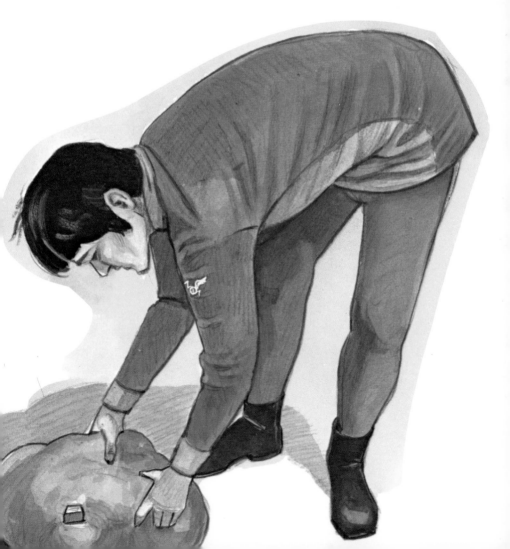

"He wants to see the Mars colony," he said. "I guess he's never been on Mars."

Joris laughed. "Maybe he thinks there'll be some more blobs here. Everybody needs a friend."

Ivo put Amorf down on a table. The soft pink blob stretched himself out into a long, liquid line. The clicking went on.

"If he isn't careful," Joris said, "he'll wear out his computer."

Ivo laughed. "He's lucky. When his brain wears out, I can always make him a new one."

"Come on," Joris urged. "You can fix that machine anytime. Take Amorf and let's go in to the colony."

"All right," Ivo agreed. "But I may not stay the whole time."

He picked up the blob and closed up his office.

They left the ship through the transition tunnel and entered the huge dome that covered the Mars colony.

"I'm always surprised when I get here," Joris said. "It looks so much like an Earth city."

Ivo nodded. "It's supposed to. It was built that way. Centuries ago, when these planet colonies

10

were planned, they didn't want the colonists to become homesick. So everything is exactly as it was on Earth."

"Maybe we should see about getting a room before we do anything else," Joris said. "Do you know where we'll find one?"

"Yes." Ivo pointed across one of the streets. "There are good living quarters over there. You can rent a room for as long as you like."

They started up the street toward the living quarters. Suddenly, there was a very loud roar. The earth shook. The huge plasticized dome that enclosed the colony rattled and swayed. The whole floor of the planet seemed to heave into the air.

Joris and Ivo were knocked flat. Amorf's computer began to click wildly. The movement stopped abruptly. Ivo picked himself up and dusted himself off. He helped Joris to his feet.

"Wow!" Joris exclaimed. "What was that?"

They looked around. People had been knocked down all over the streets. Buildings had cracked. Traffic had stopped.

"Where is headquarters?" Joris asked.

"Two streets down," Ivo said. "Let's try to find out what happened."

They ran to the headquarters building. They explained to the woman in charge who they were.

"I'm sorry," she said. "I have no time now. We must find out what happened."

She hurried away.

"We'd better get Druce," Joris said.

They rushed back to the EM 88. Druce had already left his office and was leaving the transition tunnel as they arrived.

"What was it?" Druce asked.

"It felt like an earthquake."

Dolf, the EM 88's geologist, came up behind them. "Did you feel the earthquake?" he asked.

"Are you sure that's what it was?"

"I'm positive," Dolf said. "I'm going out and see what's going on." He rushed through the tunnel.

"We tried to get some information at headquarters," Joris told Druce. "But they were too busy to speak to us."

"I'll find Tobit," Druce said. "He'll tell me what it's all about."

They went back to Mars headquarters. Tobit was not in his office.

"He is making a fast inspection tour," one of his assistants said. "I don't know what part of the colony he's at right now."

"I'm going to take a look around, too," Druce said. "I want to see if there was much damage." He suddenly turned around. "Where is your communication's room?"

The assistant showed him.

Druce stuck his head in. "Are you still in contact with Omaha headquarters?" he asked.

"Yes sir," the communicator said. "We haven't lost contact."

"Good." Druce came out. "Let's go see how much damage was done."

Out on the main street, people were wandering around. Just as Druce started to walk away, a man hurried toward him, calling his name.

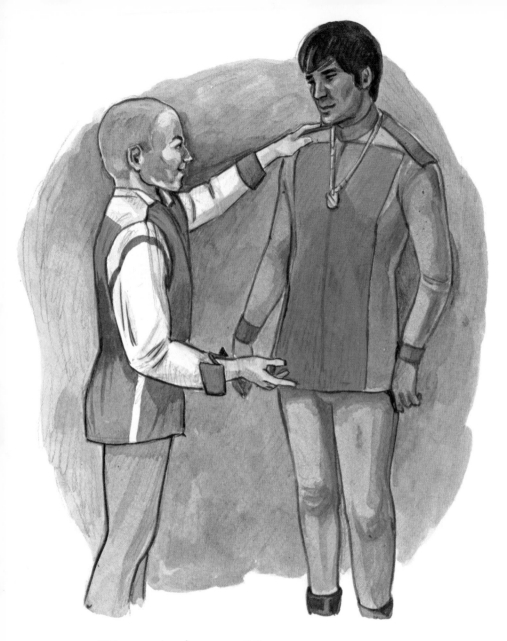

"Druce, is that you?"

"Yes, Tobit." Druce greeted the other man. "What's going on here?"

"It was an earthquake," Tobit said.

"Are you sure?" Druce asked.

Tobit nodded. "Yes. We have had small ones from time to time. But this was a major one."

"How much damage was there?" Druce asked.

"Fortunately, the dome was not damaged," Tobit said. "That's the thing that always worries us. The ground damage we can handle. But I'm concerned about our miners."

"What miners?" Joris asked.

"We have a large mining operation going on here." Tobit pointed out of the dome toward the distant mountains. "Headquarters opened a major mining field there last year," he said. "Our mountains had been mined before, but never to this extent. I'm hoping my communicator has been able to get in touch with them. They were cut off during the earthquake."

They turned and re-entered the headquarters building. Tobit went in to the communicator.

"Have you been able to get through?" he asked.

"No sir. Nothing." He pushed several buttons. "There isn't anything."

"Let us help," Druce said. "We have a geologist in our crew."

"And how about Rina?" Joris asked. "With her supersight, she could be a big help."

"And I think we should send for Galen," Ivo said. "They may need more medical help."

"We do have our own medical staff," Tobit said. "But if we have had a lot of injuries, we could probably use everyone."

"I'll go see who I can round up," Joris said.

He returned to the EM 88. Galen, the ship's doctor, packed up a bag of supplies. He decided to bring his two young assistants, Neysa and Barth, with him.

"If it's a true medical emergency," he said, "every hand will be needed."

"Dolf is already out there," Joris said. "And Rina, too. As soon as we find them, we're going up with the rescue party."

Once they had located Brita, Rina and Dolf, they prepared to join Tobit's rescue party.

"You stay with the ship, Brita," Druce ordered. "We can't both leave. I want to go along with Tobit."

They put on their spacesuits and left the safety of the giant dome. On the bare surface of Mars, movement was slower. They entered the specially

built solar carts and moved toward the distant
mountains. There was no greenery on the open
planet. The surface was rocky and pitted. The
mountains looked bare.

"They're loaded with all the natural elements," Tobit explained. "Some of our minerals are a better quality than those on the asteroids. That's why headquarters decided to start a major mining operation here. Their base camp is just ahead."

The solar cars climbed a small hill. On the other side there was a drop into a vast, bleak valley. They could see the remains of the camp.

"The center of the quake must have been near here!" Tobit exclaimed. "Everything has been leveled."

"But I don't see the miners," Druce said. "They can't have just disappeared."

"Maybe they were underground when the tremor hit," Joris said.

Dolf left the solar cart. He moved toward the center of the camp. The others followed.

"Where is the mine?" Dolf asked.

"Around the other side of this mountain," Tobit said. "We don't have to go underground. We go into the mountain itself. The mine has been in operation several years now. The men have gone quite deep inside."

The rescue party hurried around to the mine entrance.

"It's collapsed!" Rina exclaimed. "Look. You can barely see the opening."

"Look inside," Druce urged her. "Maybe with your supersight —"

Rina bent over. She stared through the small opening that was left.

"I can't see anything," she said. "Hello, there," she yelled. "Can you hear me? Hello." Her words echoed from the huge mountain.

"We have to get in there," Tobit said.

Dolf examined the entrance. "I can't tell what's inside," he said. "But the rock around the entrance is quite sturdy."

They got the special wrenches they had brought with them and reopened the entrance to the mine. Inside the main beams sagged and bulged.

"I can get in there," Ivo said. "Let me through."

"Be careful," Druce warned.

"I'm taking Amorf with me," Ivo said. "He'll go first. He can warn me if there's any danger."

Ivo laid on the ground and began to crawl through the opening. Amorf wiggled slowly ahead of him. His computer clacked his messages to Ivo.

Ivo was several hundred meters into the darkness when he suddenly heard a voice.

"Over here," it called faintly. "I'm here."

"Coming," Ivo shouted back. Quickly, he returned to the mine entrance. "Someone is alive in there," he said. "Let's clear out this entrance."

"I'm going in." Tobit pushed Ivo aside and crawled back.

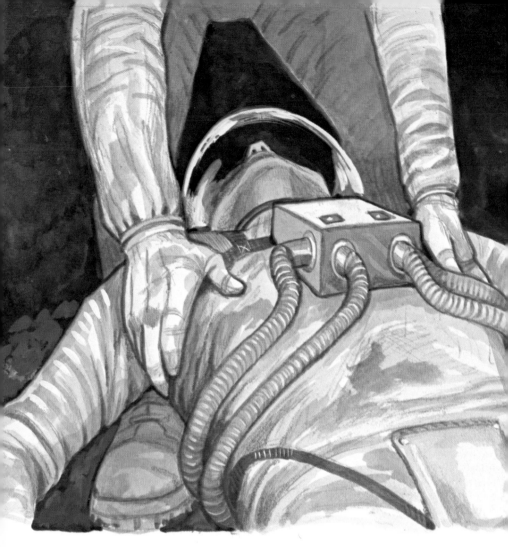

The rescue team began cleaning out the debris,
working its way slowly inside. As they built up the
crumbling walls, Tobit suddenly appeared at the far
end, bent over, tugging another man behind him.

"Where are the others?" Druce asked.

"There are four more back there," Tobit said.
"But something strange has happened to the rest of
them."

"What do you mean?"

"Let's get the others out first," Tobit said.

When the five miners had been pulled out onto the bare planet, they lay on the ground. One of them had a jagged tear in his spacesuit. Dolf quickly patched it as well as he could.

"Joris," Druce ordered, "get back to the colony. Find Galen. Get him up here as fast as you can. I don't think these miners should be moved that distance without a doctor."

While Tobit and others in the rescue party were making the injured miners more comfortable, Druce went back into the tunnel. Most of the debris had been hauled out. He was able to walk almost upright. He got to the spot where the five miners had been rescued. Beyond was a huge, black void.

"Rina," he shouted back toward the entrance. "Get in here! Bring a light with you."

Rina appeared behind him carrying a miner's beam. "What is it, Druce?" she asked. "Have you found something?"

"I don't know." Druce took the beam and peered ahead into the dark. "Take a look. You might spot something with your sight."

Rina moved carefully a few meters ahead of him. "Druce," she suddenly grabbed for his arm. "There's an enormous hole up there."

Druce stepped closer. "That's what I thought," he said. "But I can't see it clearly."

"I can," she whispered. "It looks as if it drops into nothing." She held the light down at their feet. "Let's go carefully."

They moved carefully along the narrow path. "It looks as if the whole center of the mountain is hollow," she said.

"That can't be." Druce looked around him. "A mountain is never hollow. Maybe it's just an underground cavern left from the time Mars was formed."

Rina bent over. She picked up a loose rock and tossed it into the empty blackness ahead. For a long moment there was no sound. Then from far below came a noise. It sounded like the grunt of an animal.

"Druce," Rina whispered, "there's something strange here. Let's go back."

"We'll go back," Druce said. "But only to get help and more light."

When they got back outside, Galen had arrived with his assistants, Neysa and Barth. They were giving emergency treatment to the miners.

"Load them in the cars," Tobit ordered. "We'll take them back to our hospital."

"What's in there?" Neysa asked.

"That's the mine," Druce explained.

"Can we take a look?" Barth asked.

"No," Druce said. "You can't go in there until we've examined it more closely."

"But you pulled the men out of there," Barth said.

"Do as you're told," Druce said. "Come on. Galen needs help."

As soon as the injured workers were loaded into the cars, everyone prepared to leave. Neysa suddenly looked around.

"Where is Barth?" she asked.

"He must be in one of the other cars," Galen said.

Neysa ran from one car to the other. She started into the mine's entrance.

"Neysa," Druce yelled, "come back here."

"I'll be right back." Her voice came from the opening. "Barth must have gone to —" Then there was silence.

"Those youngsters." Druce shook his head. "Rina, go and get them."

Rina ran into the tunnel. "Neysa," she called. "Barth. Come on. Let's get going."

There was no answer.

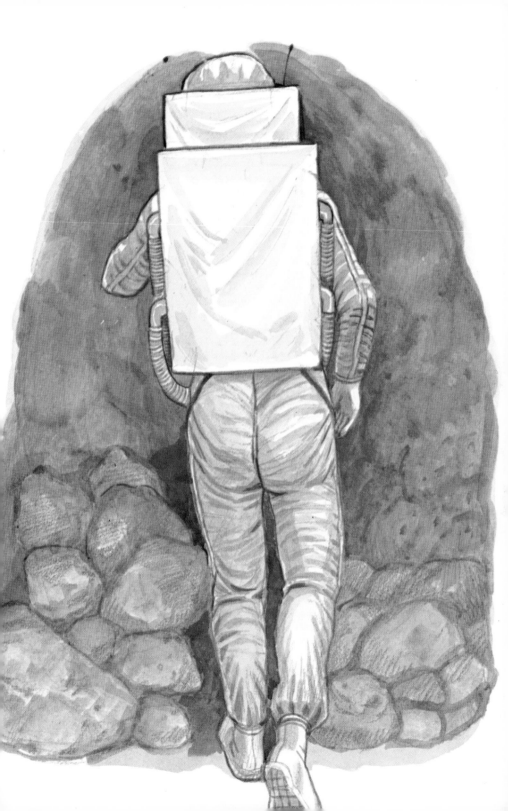

"Don't play games," she said. "We're in a hurry to get back to the dome. Will you please come out here?"

There was still no answer. Rina moved ahead carefully. She reached the edge of the path above the deep cavern. Neysa and Barth were nowhere in sight. Rina raced out of the mine.

"They're gone, Druce," she gasped. "They're not in there."

"Don't be silly," Druce said. "We saw Neysa go in."

"I know," Rina said. "But they're gone."

"You don't think —" A look of horror spread across Druce's face. "That huge cavern —"

"No — they couldn't —" Rina said. "I was in there, too. I'd have heard them fall. They've just disappeared. I don't understand it."

All of the cars had left for the dome except Druce's car. Galen and Ivo were waiting for him.

"Let me take a look in there," Ivo said.

He put Amorf up on his shoulder and picked up a light. He moved into the tunnel. The others followed closely behind him. Ivo stopped suddenly. He held a finger up to his lips. "I hear something."

There was a loud, piercing cry from the black-ness ahead.

"Druce!" a voice screamed. It was Neysa.

Then everything was quiet once more. They moved ahead carefully. They were almost to the edge of the huge black pit when they heard a strange sound on the rock below. A thud. Then Barth's voice called up.

"There are creatures down here! There are —"
Then silence.

"Creatures!" Druce exclaimed. "What can he be talking about?"

"Could there be animals?" Ivo asked.

"It's impossible," Galen said. "There is no natural animal life on Mars. Nothing could survive without oxygen."

"No." Rina's eyes looked like large, glowing stones in the dark. "But maybe there is something native to the planet that we don't know about."

"That can't be." Galen's voice was loud and sure. "We've had a colony on Mars for centuries. If there were any creatures, someone would have seen them by now."

"How many lights do we have?" Druce asked.

"Three," Ivo said. "Why?"

"Ivo, do you have anything with you that we can put down in the hole that will light it?"

Galen looked through his bag. "Maybe I have," he said, "a piece of tubing, or —"

"Good. We will put one light on the tubing. What else can we use?"

"I know," Ivo suddenly said. "We have Amorf. It won't be the first time we've used him like this."

He attached one of the lights to the blob.

"All right, Amorf," he said. "I want you to stretch yourself as thin as you can. I want you to go all the way down that hole."

Both lights were lowered as far as they could go, Ivo's dropping farther than the one on the tubing.

Rina gasped. "There are creatures!" she cried. "Look!"

"I can't see," Druce said. "It's still too — the shadows —"

"There!" Rina was staring, her supersight easily picking out the huddled creatures along the cavern wall. "They have Neysa and Barth," she said.

"What are they?" Druce asked.

"They're men," Rina said. "That is, they look like men. But they're different."

"What do you mean, different?"

"Covered with hair," she said. "But I think — yes — I think they're beards — and their hair is down to the floor — and —"

"Are they dressed?" Ivo asked.

"Yes, in something strange. I can't make out what it is. They're covered with something that looks almost like mud."

"Mud!"

"And some kind of strange leaf."

"We have to get down there," Druce said. "Barth, Neysa, can you hear us?"

Rina stared into the cavern. "They're shaking their heads. But they're being held. They can't answer."

34

"How are we going to get down there?" Galen asked.

"I have a feeling," Druce said, "if one of us started down, it might scare the creatures away."

"You're right," Rina said. "They look frightened now."

"Then let's start a human ladder. Rina, you sit on my feet. Galen, take my hands. Ivo, you grab on to Galen. Then drop Amorf with the light as far down as you can."

The ladder was quickly formed. As Ivo dropped to the black cavern, he swung Amorf and the light from side to side. He could see the creatures clearly himself now. They were, indeed, men. When the light and the pink blob swung toward them, the two holding Neysa and Barth let go and ran.

"Can you get to me?" Ivo called.

Neysa and Barth raced toward him. He swung them one at a time up over his shoulder so they could crawl back to the top. They were both crying.

"It was awful," Neysa sobbed. "They smelled. And they were rough. And —"

"But they spoke our language," Barth said. "It was very strange. They understood us."

"They understood you!" Druce exclaimed. "Then they aren't creatures from another world. They have to be some kind of lost man."

"Let's get you two back to the dome," Galen

said. "I want to examine you."

They got into the solar cart and raced back to the Mars' colony.

When Neysa and Barth had gotten cleaned up, they met with the others in Tobit's office.

"They were certainly men," Neysa said. "There's no question about that."

"But it's not possible," Galen said. "Man cannot survive in this atmosphere. They had no spacesuits."

"Somehow they're a species who have developed here."

"And they speak our language? I don't believe it," Druce declared. "Are you missing any colonists?" he asked Tobit.

"Of course not," Tobit said. "It would have been reported to headquarters long ago. Wait." A strange look suddenly came over his face.

He rushed to a computer in the corner and pushed several buttons quickly.

"What is that?" Druce asked as Tobit came toward them with a sheet of paper.

39

"The history of this colony," Tobit said. "I suddenly remembered. You know, we don't go back and forth the way you people do," he explained. "I mean, you people who are on space duty return to Earth when your tour is finished. Those of us in the colonies stay here forever. We've been here many generations." He held out the paper from the computer. "I remember hearing a story. A group of workers were mining here hundreds of years ago. There was an earthquake. A bad one. So bad that our historians refer to it as 'the quake.' That mountain" — he pointed to the one where the mining operation had taken place — "that mountain was formed from the center of the planet. At that time, a group of miners disappeared. It was assumed they had been killed in the quake. No trace of them was ever found."

"But they couldn't still be alive," Rina said. "Not if it was hundreds of years ago."

"I'm going back there," Druce said. "Where is Dolf? I want him with me."

"I'm going too," Rina said. "I'm the only one who can see where we're going."

They put a party together quickly and rushed back to the mine. They were equipped with long metal coiled ropes and powerful solar lights. As they came to the entrance, they heard the sound of movement below.

Rina held up her hand for silence. "There's someone ahead of us on the path," she whispered. She pointed directly ahead.

Dolf made a running jump. He landed on a soft body in front of him. He tackled the creature to the ground. When he wrestled him to his feet, he stared. The creature was human. But he looked ancient. His skin was dark and wrinkled. Hair grew wildly from his head, his eyebrows and his face.

Druce hurried over. He held up his light. "Who are you?" he asked.

"Vark," the creature said. He tried to shrink back against the wall.

"Do you live here?" Druce asked.

"Live down." Vark pointed to the hole.

"How many of you are there?" Druce asked.

"Many, many," Vark said. He looked toward the tunnel where the light was coming in the entrance. He held his hand up before his eyes.

"Haven't you ever seen light before?" Druce asked.

Vark shook his head.

Dolf stepped forward. "Captain," he said, "I think I know what happened here. It's going to sound like the strangest thing you've ever heard. But they must have been trapped at the time of the terrible earthquake. His ancestors, I mean. These people have been living underground for hundreds of years."

"But that's not possible," Druce said. "What have they survived on? There's no food."

"We don't know that," Dolf said. He turned to Vark. "Eat. What do you eat?"

Vark didn't seem to understand.

Dolf made the motion of eating with his hand and his mouth.

A look of understanding spread across Vark's face. He pointed down the hole. "Fed," he said. "Fed."

"That must mean food. Tallu once told us that there was water under some of the planets," Druce exclaimed. "He was talking about Venus, not Mars. But it must be the same thing here. There must be water at the center of the planet. Which means there are probably plants that grow and water to drink," Druce added. "That's how they've survived."

"But the spacesuits," Rina said. "I don't understand."

"I do," Dolf said. "Until now, they've been sealed off completely from the atmosphere. It probably took a few generations, but now they've adapted completely. They could probably even walk outside now without anything happening."

"You mean it's as if they were living in their own space capsule there," Rina said.

"That's right." Dolf nodded. "And their bodies have adapted to what little atmosphere did seep in. Now, they're able to survive completely. I would like to take this one back with us if we can, Druce," Dolf said. "Can you imagine Galen's face when he sees Vark?"

"How do we tell him that we're friends? . . . That we won't hurt him?" Rina asked.

"That's easy." Ivo came up to Vark and picked up his hand.

Vark shrank farther back along the wall. Ivo shook his hand. Vark snatched his hand away.

"I think it has to be stronger than that," Druce said. He gave a little laugh.

He put his arm around Vark and hugged him. He smiled. Vark looked at him cautiously.

"Vark, call your people." Druce motioned for the others to come up.

Vark stared at him for a long moment. Suddenly, he leaned over into the cavern and gave a loud, blood-curdling yell.

A swarm of people came up the side. Some were children. Most were adults.

"Come with us," Druce said. "Out there." He pointed toward the light.

Vark turned to the others. "Out," he said. "Out."

Some of the creatures went to the entrance. They grabbed at their eyes and turned away.

"They're afraid of the light," Ivo said. "How will we get them out?"

Vark stepped forward. "We go," he said. He turned to the rest of his people.

"We come with bang," he said. "Now is other bang. Is time to go."

Druce nodded. "Vark is right. They were trapped by an earthquake. Now an earthquake has freed
them. Somehow that only seems right."

He turned and led them out of the mountain.